FOREVER
AMIGO

AN ABBY STORY

Book design by Jake Nordby
Illustrations by Jomike Tejido

Published in the United States by Jolly Fish Press, an imprint of North Star Editions, Inc.

First Edition
First Printing, 2018

Library of Congress Cataloging-in-Publication Data
Names: Abrams, Kelsey, author. | Tejido, Jomike, illustrator.
Title: Forever Amigo : an Abby story / Kelsey Abrams ; illustrated by Jomike Tejido.
Description: Mendota Heights, MN : Jolly Fish Press, [2019] | Series: Second Chance Ranch | Summary: "Abby struggles with the loss of her service dog, Amigo"—Provided by publisher.
Identifiers: LCCN 2018032140 (print) | LCCN 2018039490 (ebook) | ISBN 9781631632570 (e-book) | ISBN 9781631632563 (pbk.) | ISBN 9781631632556 (hardcover)
Subjects: | CYAC: Dogs—Fiction. | Service dogs—Fiction. | Grief—Fiction. | Autism—Fiction. | Grief—Fiction. | Sisters—Fiction. | Ranch life—Fiction. | Hispanic Americans—Fiction.
Classification: LCC PZ7.1.A18 (ebook) | LCC PZ7.1.A18 Fo 2019 (print) | DDC [Fic]—dc23
LC record available at https://lccn.loc.gov/2018032140

Jolly Fish Press
North Star Editions, Inc.
2297 Waters Drive
Mendota Heights, MN 55120
www.jollyfishpress.com

Printed in the United States of America

SECOND CHANCE
RANCH

FOREVER
AMIGO

AN ABBY STORY

KELSEY ABRAMS

ILLUSTRATED BY JOMIKE TEJIDO

TEXT BY WHITNEY SANDERSON

JOLLY
FiSH
PRESS

Mendota Heights, Minnesota

Chapter One

Abby jumped down from the school bus steps and raced up the long driveway to the farmhouse on the hill. "Bye! Thanks, Ms. Bea!" she remembered to call back to the bus driver. Her backpack seemed to feel lighter with every step she took.

Abby didn't dislike school, exactly, but it made her feel tired. The day was long and filled with one challenge after another. Loud bells, sudden changes from one subject to the next, and waiting in line. So much waiting in line.

And then there were the other kids . . . If only they were as easy to understand as the word problems in math class. For those, you just had to figure out what the question was really asking, write it down as an equation, and solve it. No problem. But there was no equation for working out people problems, and it seemed like the rules were always changing.

For example, why did her maybe-friends Cora, Cat, and Savannah invite her to ride bikes with them yesterday and act like they barely knew her today? Why did her definitely-friend Miriam get so grumpy when Abby said Miriam's new glasses made her look like John Lennon? Miriam loved the classic rock group the Beatles. Why wouldn't she want to look like one of their lead singers?

Most of all, why did Abby's usually annoying class-mate Jamal help her pick up the stack of library books she'd dropped on the stairs? Sure, she'd only dropped them in the first place because he'd bumped into her, but usually, he would have just raced off without even apologizing.

Abby left all these questions behind as she entered the spacious ranch house. She dropped off her backpack at her unloading dock near the mudroom door and left her shoes there too. She always kept her stuff in the same place so she wouldn't lose track of it in the rush to get ready for school. With three sisters close to her own age, mornings in the Ramirez household could be pretty chaotic. She knew she was going to be home alone this afternoon for a few hours. Her dad had taken Emily and Grace to their dentist appointments, her mom was still at work, and Natalie's school didn't get out until later.

"Amigo, I'm home!" she called out. But it wasn't necessary. Amigo was already hurrying in from his favorite spot in the living room—well, as much as he hurried these days.

Like Abby, Amigo was ten years old. For dogs, this was pretty old, around the age of Abby's grand-parents. Not long ago, Abby had come home to find Amigo missing from the house. It turned out, there was a problem with his heart and he had to be taken to the animal hospital where her mom worked as a veterinarian.

Mrs. Ramirez had prescribed Amigo medicine for his heart condition. It was Abby's job to give him the pills with his breakfast every morning. She did everything for Amigo. Until recently, Amigo had gone to school with her as her service dog for autism. He was trained to help her in several different ways if she started to get stressed out or overwhelmed. But he was mostly retired now, and he only went to school with Abby if she was having a really bad day.

Amigo came over and licked Abby's hands, his fringed golden-brown tail waving in the air. He was a golden retriever, a breed known for its friendly temperament and trainability. Amigo had originally been trained as a service dog for another child. Unfortunately, that boy had been very sick and had died from his illness. Amigo had gone back to the Helping Paws Center where he had originally been trained. Abby had picked him out right away when her family had gone there to find her a service dog.

That had been four years ago. Since then, Abby could count on one hand the times she and Amigo had been apart for more than a day.

"Who's the best dog in the world?" asked Abby as Amigo came over to greet her. Amigo tossed his head and pranced in place. He knew it was him.

Abby stroked Amigo's silky fur and told him how much she'd missed him while she was at school. He followed her as she went over to the side of the refrigerator to look at the magnetic dry-erase board stuck to the side.

It was her schedule board. At the top, the date was written in purple marker. Each hour of the day was marked off with its own square. All her activities were written into the squares. Now it was just past three o'clock, and the next item on the list was "Have a snack." Next to the words was a hand-drawn picture of a peanut butter and jelly sandwich and a glass of juice. Somehow, seeing a picture next to the words made everything clearer and easier to remember.

Abby poured her juice and made her sandwich, saving the cut-off crusts for Daisy, the Berkshire pig. She was grateful the ranch had rescued a pig, who could eat all kinds of table scraps.

Amigo looked wistfully at the crusts. He loved peanut butter. But the bread and jelly weren't very healthy for dogs, and Amigo had his own treats. Abby got out a box of dog biscuits from the cupboard and gave Amigo two of them while she ate her own snack.

"Want to go for a walk, buddy?" she asked when she had finished. Instead of jumping up and grabbing his leash in his mouth like he usually did, Amigo just wagged his tail politely and heaved a little sigh.

Abby sighed too. Lately, Amigo hadn't had as

much energy as usual. He still liked to go for walks, but he hardly ever ran or played like he used to.

As Abby rinsed her plate in the sink, she thought about the rest of her day. The next item on her list just said "AMIGO!" Abby reserved an hour after school every day just to spend time with him. Her sister Emily had drawn the picture of Amigo that went next to his name. Abby was pretty good at drawing, but Emily was better.

After "AMIGO!," the next activity in her day was "Dog chores." Abby was in charge of looking after the ranch's rescued dogs. The ranch had just had a big adoption event, so there was only one rescued dog now. She was a one-year-old black Labrador named Bella. She was still just a big puppy, and she had lots of energy.

Maybe combining Bella's playtime with Amigo's would help perk him up. Amigo often ended up being almost like a teacher to some of the younger dogs at the ranch. Dogs learned from each other as much as they learned from people. Not long ago, Amigo had helped a fearful German shepherd named Destiny trust people more. Now Destiny had a new home with Miriam's older brother, Caleb.

Abby headed to the kennel room at the far end of the house on the first floor. Inside the large room were some crates, a metal grooming table, and a playpen for young puppies. Outside, in the middle of a row of long chain-link pens, a glossy black dog was lying in the grass, chewing on a rope toy.

The dog sprang to her feet when she saw Abby. Her tail wagged so hard, it made her whole hind end sway back and forth.

"Hi, Bella," said Abby, smiling. It was hard not to feel cheerful around such a happy dog. Even though Bella had been found abandoned in a shopping mall parking lot, she almost never seemed sad or worried.

Abby opened the gate to Bella's pen and clipped a leash on her collar. She led Bella into the house. When Bella spotted Amigo, she sank into a playful bow. Amigo touched noses with Bella and sniffed her all over. His tail started to wag slowly and then faster.

Abby led them both outside to the ranch's big backyard. She found a tennis ball in the grass and threw it as far as she could. Bella ran after it, but Amigo lay down in the grass under the big, shady oak tree. Abby felt a little disappointed. She'd hoped that Bella's energy would encourage Amigo to play.

Bella brought back the ball and dropped it at Abby's feet. Abby threw it for her again. She bounded away through the grass, barking with delight. This time when she came back, she dropped the tennis ball at Amigo's feet.

He looked curiously at it for a moment, then lifted his paw and rolled the ball toward Bella. The young dog snapped it up in her mouth and galloped in a

circle around him. Amigo got stiffly to his feet, then started loping after her.

"That's the spirit, Amigo!" exclaimed Abby.

Bella brought the tennis ball back to Abby again. She held the now slightly soggy green ball in one hand.

"Sit, Bella," she said.

Bella's tail wagged at the sound of her name, but otherwise, she didn't move.

"Sit," Abby repeated. She pushed gently on Bella's hindquarters until Bella sat down. "Good girl!" she said, tossing Bella the ball as a reward.

Bella romped in a little victory lap and came back for another round. Abby asked Bella to sit again. This time, Bella sank down onto her haunches all by herself.

"Good sit!" said Abby enthusiastically before throwing the ball again.

Bella caught the ball in her mouth and tossed her head up and down to show it off, her floppy ears splaying in all directions.

Bella's really smart, Abby thought. *I don't think even Amigo learned commands that fast.*

Abby looked around to see where Amigo was. For a moment, she couldn't find him. Then she saw him stretched out motionless in the grass a short distance away, his eyes closed.

"Amigo!" Abby shouted. But he didn't respond.

Chapter Two

Amigo lay on the cold metal table in the vet's office. Electrodes were attached to a shaved area on his chest. Across the room, Mrs. Ramirez watched a digital display that showed Amigo's heartbeat as a series of colored lines moving across a black screen.

Abby stood next to Amigo, stroking his head. In her mind, she could still see the awful image of him lying so still in the grass. He hadn't woken up even when she'd called his name and shaken him.

She'd had to leave him lying on the grass while she ran inside to call her mom at the office. When she got back outside, Amigo was sitting up and looking around. Bella was lying next to Amigo, licking his fur and nudging him with her nose like she was trying to comfort him.

By the time Mrs. Ramirez got there, Amigo had seemed almost normal. He'd even picked up the tennis ball and started chewing on it. But Mrs. Ramirez had brought him to the clinic for some tests anyway. Just like last time . . . Abby was starting to hate the sight of the low, square white building, even though it was filled with animals and the people trying to help them.

"What's wrong with Amigo?" asked Abby, her hand

still resting protectively on Amigo's head. She looked intently at her mother as she waited for an answer, but Amigo was looking up at Abby.

"Amigo had a heart attack," said Mrs. Ramirez, leaving the monitor and coming over to them. "That means something was stopping the blood from pumping through his heart. It could have been a blood clot or a problem with the nerves in his heart."

"Is it the same thing that happened before?" asked Abby. Mrs. Ramirez had said Amigo's problem was with his heart last time, but she hadn't explained more. Abby had been too upset to listen, anyway. She just knew she had to give him his pills every day, and she never missed a dose.

"Yes," said Mrs. Ramirez. "This is the same thing. Luckily, Amigo recovered before, and I think he'll be okay this time too."

Abby put her arms around Amigo's neck and hugged him tightly. She wished she could share her own heart with him or give him a new one. "What can we do to stop it from happening again?" she asked.

"Amigo already gets medicine to thin his blood," said Mrs. Ramirez. "I can add an anti-inflammatory pill that might help."

Abby nodded. Amigo was so good about taking his pills. A lot of dogs tried to spit them out or run away when they saw the bottle, but Amigo seemed to know they were meant to help him.

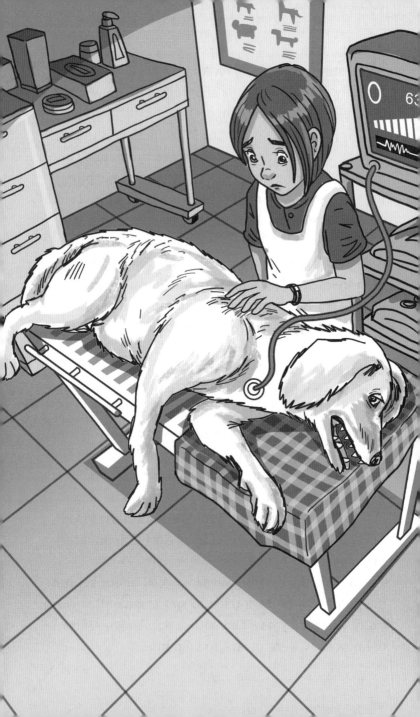

"The activity of running around the yard could have triggered his heart attack, so we'll have to be careful to keep him quiet and calm," Mrs. Ramirez added.

She put her hand on Amigo's back and said gently, "Amigo's had a long life and a good one. We need to prepare ourselves for the fact that he's not going to be with us forever."

Abby wasn't listening. She was already thinking of everything she could do for Amigo. "I can sleep downstairs next to his bed in the living room, so he won't have to climb the stairs to my room," she said. "I can even bring him his breakfast in bed, like you do when I'm sick."

Mrs. Ramirez smiled. "That's thoughtful of you, but it won't be necessary. Amigo can still go upstairs for now and even go for walks like he usually does. It will be good for him to keep up his daily activities for as long as possible. We just need to be careful that he doesn't overexert himself."

"I guess he can't play with Bella anymore," said Abby. She felt mad at herself for not realizing that a combined play session would be too much for Amigo. She wouldn't make the same mistake again.

Amigo meant everything to Abby, and she would do whatever he needed to help him get well.

🐾

Abby clutched her lunch bag tightly as she looked around for a place to sit in the busy cafeteria. She usually sat with Miriam, but Miriam was absent from school because she was visiting her grandmother's house for Yom Kippur.

Abby noticed an empty seat at a table filled with other kids from her class, including Jamal. She kept looking. The only other seats were at tables full of little kids. She wished she could sit with Grace and Emily, but they ate lunch at a different time.

Reluctantly, Abby walked over and sat down in front of the only empty seat at the table—next to Jamal.

"What's up, Tabby Abby?" he asked, popping open his carton of chocolate milk and pouring it into his mouth from about a foot above.

Abby jerked away to avoid being splashed by brown droplets.

Jamal loved to make up nicknames for her. He seemed to think it was the height of humor. So one day, she was Gabby Abby, and the next, she was Scabby Abby. Or Flabby Abby. Or Crabby Abby. Before she met Jamal, Abby had never realized that so many words rhymed with her name.

" 'Tabby,' because you like animals, get it?" asked Jamal.

"I get it," said Abby.

Jamal meowed like a cat. The other kids at the

table laughed. Abby rolled her eyes. He pretended to paw at his own tail, and his friends laughed even harder. He swatted Abby's packet of crackers across the table.

"Quit it, Jamal," muttered Abby, getting up to retrieve the crackers. She was starting to wish she had sat at the table full of first-graders.

"I'm just *horsing around*, Abby. Get it?" Jamal whinnied and started acting like a bucking bronco as Abby settled back into her seat. His flying elbow hit Abby's juice box and knocked it into her lap.

Abby gasped, cringing at the feeling of cold liquid soaking into her clothes. She looked down in dismay at the purple blot spreading across the fabric.

"Look what you did, Jamal!" she cried. "Ugh, now my favorite skirt has a grape juice stain!"

"Hey, don't have a cow," said Jamal, piling paper napkins onto her lap. "A cow, because you like animals, get—"

Abby stood up. Napkins fluttered to the floor, and juice dripped into her socks.

"YES, I GET IT!" she yelled. "I JUST DON'T THINK IT'S FUNNY!"

She got up, grabbed the remains of her lunch, and stalked out of the cafeteria, ignoring the stares of the other students. She went into the bathroom and tried to wash off her skirt, but the water just made the stain bigger.

Leaving the bathroom, she continued down the hall, past the rows of coat hooks, and flopped down onto the chill-out chair outside the school counselor's office. Abby was allowed to sit there if she needed a short break from class. She definitely needed one now.

A moment later, the office door opened, and the

guidance counselor, LeeAnn, stepped out into the hall with an empty coffee mug in one hand.

"Is everything okay, Abby?" LeeAnn asked, noticing her there.

"No," said Abby, crossing her arms tightly over her chest. "I just spilled grape juice on my favorite skirt, Jamal Parker is always bugging me, and Amigo had a heart attack yesterday."

"Oh, I'm so sorry to hear that, Abby," said LeeAnn. "Do you want to come into my office and talk about it?"

"No," said Abby. LeeAnn was good at helping to solve some problems, but she couldn't make Amigo better, she couldn't help with her skirt now, and she probably couldn't make Jamal less annoying. "I should go back to class now."

"If you want to talk later, you know where to find me," said LeeAnn.

Abby got up from the chill-out chair and started to walk back to her classroom, her feet dragging with every step.

Maybe next year I can be homeschooled, she thought hopefully. But she knew her parents didn't really have time for that, and Abby wasn't sure it was really what she wanted anyway. She'd miss Miriam and her teacher, Mr. Timothy. He had an Airedale terrier named Jazz, and he often showed funny YouTube videos to go along with his lessons. It was amazing how much easier it was to remember the elements on the periodic table when someone was rapping about them.

Abby entered the classroom and slipped into her seat. Math class had just started. She tried to pay attention to what Mr. Timothy was saying about plotting graphs, but she had already read that chapter in her workbook, and her thoughts kept drifting to Amigo.

What was he doing now? Does he miss me? Was he feeling better yet? Abby kept her eye on the round wall clock above Mr. Timothy's head, counting the minutes until she would see Amigo again.

Chapter Three

After what seemed like an almost endless day, the final bell rang. Abby groaned when she remembered that her name was on the list for classroom cleanup that day. Quickly, she helped Mr. Timothy sweep up the spilled potting soil and bits of leaves from their terrarium project.

Everyone's finished terrariums sat on a sunny shelf by the window. In hers, which was really a glass fishbowl, Abby had planted Texas bluebonnet, lemon mint, buffalo grass, and a plumeria seed that Natalie's friend Darcy had brought back from Hawai'i.

"I'm not sure if plumeria will grow in a terrarium with soil and plants from Texas," Abby said to Mr. Timothy.

"We'll find out soon," he said with a smile.

Usually, Abby liked to ask Mr. Timothy for stories about Jazz, but today, she rushed through her task as fast as she could, checking the floor for dropped pencils and helping to wipe the whiteboard clean.

When she had finished helping Mr. Timothy tidy up the room, she headed out into the hall to grab her backpack. She saw Cora, Cat, and Savannah standing in a group by Cora's hook, which was near Abby's.

The three of them were talking about a movie

that Abby hadn't seen yet. They glanced up when they saw her, but they didn't say anything.

"Hi," said Abby. "Do you want to ride bikes together again this afternoon? I have to go home and take care of Amigo now, but I could meet you at the park later."

Cora, Cat, and Savannah exchanged glances, somehow all at once. Expressions crossed their faces too fast for Abby to figure out what they meant.

"Um, maybe some other time," said Savannah, fidgeting with the hair scrunchie around her wrist.

"How about tomorrow?" asked Abby.

"How about ten past never?" Cat whispered into Cora's ear, but loudly enough that Abby could hear.

Abby was confused. *Ten past never?* How could it be ten minutes past a time that doesn't exist? Does that mean they never want to ride bikes with me again?

Abby was still trying to figure things out when Cora tugged on Cat's sleeve. "Come on, let's go wait for the bus outside, where it's less . . . awkward," she said. Cat grabbed her backpack, giggling and shooting a glance back in Abby's direction.

Only Savannah stayed where she was. But she kept edging away a little bit at a time, like she was connected to her friends by an invisible elastic band that was stretching tighter and tighter.

"Um . . . I just wanted to tell you that Cat and

Cora decided not to ask you to ride bikes with us today because they think you're weird," she said in a rush.

Abby stared at her. She didn't know if Savannah was being mean or not. She searched the other girl's face for clues. Savannah's eyes were fixed on a wad of bubblegum smashed to the floor. She wasn't smirking, and she didn't look angry. She was biting her lip.

"Why do they think I'm weird?" Abby finally asked.

"You know, because of how you talk," said Savannah to the wad of bubblegum.

"How do I talk?"

"Like that," said Savannah. "Like, even when you ask a question, it doesn't really sound like a question, you know?"

Abby didn't know. Whenever she heard herself talking out loud, it sounded normal to her.

"After you rode bikes with us, Cora and Cat kept repeating stuff that you said," Savannah went on. "They thought you might say more funny stuff if you hung out with us again, but I said it would be mean."

"What did I say that they were repeating?" asked Abby. She tried as hard as she could to make it sound like a question.

"Um, I don't really want to say," said Savannah, blushing. "Cora and Cat can be kind of mean sometimes. More than they realize. Anyway, I don't think you sound *that* different . . . just a little bit."

"Oh," said Abby. She didn't know what else to say.

"Well, I just thought you should know," said Savannah. Abby thought she looked unhappy, but she didn't know why. Abby was the one who Cora and Cat had been laughing at.

Savannah turned and hurried away down the hall. Abby stayed in the hall, rearranging the stuff in her backpack until she was sure all three of them were gone.

Usually, Abby felt a sense of satisfaction when she solved for the missing number in an equation. Except this time, the number came out to negative three.

As in, three people who were definitely not her friends.

🐾

Later that afternoon, Abby sat at the kitchen table with a blank sheet of paper in front of her. She was trying to focus on her homework and not her school day, but it was difficult. Savannah's words kept echoing in Abby's head, almost as clearly as if she'd just said them.

Abby wondered if other people thought she talked funny too. She wondered if sometimes, when she said something that made Miriam laugh, Miriam was actually laughing *at* her and not *with* her. How could she tell the difference?

Amigo lay by her feet, his head resting on his

paws. He hadn't felt like going for a walk, so Abby had just let him lie out in the sunny yard and brushed his golden fur until it was silky smooth and free from tangles.

Abby had made her usual snack, but Amigo hadn't wanted his two biscuits. He'd just sniffed them and turned his head away. She couldn't resist sneaking him a bite of her sandwich instead. He hadn't been able to say no to that.

Abby drummed her fingers on the table as she reread the instructions for her science homework. She had to make an illustration of a woodland ecosystem. Emily had lent Abby her art set with two hundred fifty colored pencils in almost every imaginable shade. Abby looked carefully at all the different varieties of green before choosing one that looked the most like the color of an oak leaf.

As she worked, Abby balanced each colored pencil upright with its flat end on the table after she used it. Then she got an idea and started standing every pencil in the set on its end, creating a spiral shape. The wide end of the spiral started with red, pink, and orange. Then it narrowed to yellow, green, blue, indigo, and deep purple in the middle.

Half an hour later, when she had placed the last pencil, Abby stood back and admired her work. From above, the pointy tips of the pencils made a beautiful pattern of rainbow dots. From the side, it looked like

a multicolored forest. Maybe Emily would want to take a photograph of it.

"Hello? Anybody home?" Grace came bursting into the kitchen so suddenly that even sleepy Amigo jumped. She was wearing her soccer cleats, which she hadn't taken off in the mudroom, even though their mom was always reminding Grace that they scuffed up the floor.

"Wow, cool!" Grace said, her eyes widening when she saw the pencil spiral. She tossed the soccer ball she was holding aside, and it bounced away into a corner of the room. She sat down at the table across from Abby and grabbed a sheet of paper.

"My coach said I should practice visualizing a good game," she said. "I'm going to draw myself scoring a goal." She reached toward the spiral for a blue colored pencil that was the color of her team's shirt.

Abby opened her mouth to say, "No!"

But before the word came out, Grace's hand jostled the edge of the pencil spiral. The navy-blue colored pencil clattered onto its side, tipping into the sky blue and the robin's egg blue and the turquoise and the light green . . . In a few noisy seconds, the entire spiral was an ugly, mixed-up heap.

Abby felt a rush of anger. "You're so careless, Grace!" she yelled. "You ruin everything!"

Amigo, hearing Abby's raised voice, jumped to his feet and nudged her hand. It was his reminder to her that she was getting upset.

Grace's forehead crinkled into a scowl. "It was an accident!" she said. "You don't have to be so mean about it."

"I'm not being mean," said Abby. "I'm being honest." She was still annoyed, but she didn't want to upset Amigo anymore, so she forced herself to keep her voice low.

Amigo settled back down onto the floor, glancing worriedly from Abby to Grace and back again.

"No, you're being a jerk!" Grace shot back. "Emily wouldn't get so upset, and it's her art set. Even bossy pants Natalie is nicer to me than you are."

"Then maybe you should go mess up something Emily or Natalie is doing," Abby snapped.

Grace jumped up from the table, grabbed her soccer ball, and stormed out of the room. Abby looked at the heap of pencils in front of her and let out a growl of frustration. *What a mess!*

Amigo stood up to nudge her hand again. Abby patted him absently, then she shook her head and focused her attention on him.

"You're right, Amigo. There's no point in getting worked up," she said. Amigo licked her hand, and Abby smiled as she started to clean up the colored pencils.

No matter how bad her day was going, Amigo always knew how to make her feel better.

Chapter Four

On Saturday morning, Abby saw a note on the refrigerator door: "Abby or Natalie—We are out of rabbit food again. Can one of you please walk to Jackson's Feed Store and get some? xo Mom."

Abby knew her dad was at Grace's soccer game and Emily had plans with her new friend, Oliver. And her mom was at the office. She didn't always work on the weekends, but the clinic was open one Saturday a month, and today was that day. But where was Natalie?

Abby looked out the window and saw Natalie riding one of the rescue horses in the arena. Their teenage neighbor, Marco, was riding with her. Either she hadn't seen the note, or she had left it on purpose for Abby.

Either way, Abby was going to have to get the rabbit food herself. She had been planning to take Amigo for a walk, but she could do both tasks at once. Amigo liked going to the feed store. The owner, Mr. Jackson, always gave Amigo a homemade jerky strip so he could show off his favorite trick.

But would walking the mile to the store be too much for Amigo? Abby called her mom to ask.

"No, bringing Amigo is a good idea," said her

mother. "He should get a little bit of exercise, and going into town might lift his spirits."

Amigo had spent a lot of time on his fleecy bed in the living room over the past few days. He was there now, and Abby called to him from the kitchen. She heard the sound of him yawning, and then a little groan as he stretched.

After a moment, he came tip-tapping into the kitchen. His strides were stiff and slow, but his eyes were bright.

Abby made sure she walked slowly along the dusty road to town, pausing to give Amigo plenty of chances to rest.

Mr. Jackson was at the front of the store when they walked in, talking to a young woman wearing tall riding boots. They were standing in front of an assortment of horse bridles hanging on the wall, discussing the pros and cons of each one.

Abby didn't want to bother them, so she led Amigo past them to the back aisle of the shop, where the animal feed was stored. The bags of rabbit food were up on a high shelf near the ceiling, way above Abby's head.

She glanced across the store at Mr. Jackson. He was still talking to the other customer, and Abby felt too shy to interrupt them. Looking around, she spotted a big can of birdseed. She pushed it across the floor toward the shelves. Then she looped Amigo's leash around a nearby display of garden rakes and scrambled on top of the container.

The lid wasn't perfectly flat, so Abby teetered on the domed metal surface until she got her balance and then stood up. She pulled at the five-pound bag of rabbit food that she wanted on the top shelf. It was underneath some heavier twenty-pound sacks, and she wiggled the corner back and forth as she tried to work it free.

Amigo let out a sharp, sudden bark of warning.

"What's wrong, buddy?" asked Abby, turning to look at him. The worry wrinkles on his forehead had crinkled deeper. He barked at her again.

"I'll be down in a second," she said. She turned back around and tugged harder on the bag of rabbit food. Suddenly, not just that bag but *all* of them were sliding toward her!

One of the twenty-pound bags hit Abby's shoulder, knocking her off-balance. She felt the can topple beneath her as she fell to the ground. *Thud! Thud! Thud!* Bags of rabbit food rained down from the shelf like bombs falling from the sky.

Abby clasped her arms over her head for protection and tucked her knees up to her bent forehead. She felt herself rocking back and forth as the world spun dizzily around her. All she could hear clearly was the pounding of her own heart.

Then a low "Woof!" sounded close to her ear, and

a weight settled onto her lap. She felt Amigo's paw pressing into her leg. The pressure helped to bring her back to the moment. She lowered her arms and looked around.

The metal can was laying on its side, and an ocean of pale-yellow birdseed covered the floor. Bags of rabbit food were scattered all around.

Abby heard her own name, and Mr. Jackson's face came into focus above her. He had a long mustache that made Abby think of a character in an old cowboy movie.

"Are you in one piece, Abby?" he asked. "That was quite a tumble."

Abby guided Amigo off her legs. When she got very frightened, he was trained to lie down on her lap. The weight of his body helped to focus and ground her. Now he rose and backed a few paces away, giving her space to get up. Abby moved her arms and legs. Nothing hurt.

"I'm okay," said Abby, standing slowly. "Sorry about the birdseed. I can help clean it up."

"No need for that. It'll give Dylan something to do other than send text messages to his friends," said Mr. Jackson with a smile. Dylan was his teenage nephew who worked part-time at the store. "But next time, ask for help if you need something on a shelf," he added. "A bag of rabbit food isn't worth a concussion!"

Abby picked up one of the fallen bags and carried it over to the checkout counter with Amigo close behind her. Mr. Jackson put the cost on her parents' account. Because the Ramirez family shopped at the store so often, Mr. Jackson just sent a bill at the end of every month.

As they stood in front of the high, old-fashioned wooden counter, Amigo eyed the glass jar of home-made jerky treats next to the cash register. He was too polite to beg, but Abby could see his entire attention focused on the jar.

Mr. Jackson noticed too. "And what can I get for you today, sir?" he asked. He liked to talk to Amigo like he was a customer. "Oh, right away. One piece of venison jerky coming right up." He took the lid off the jar and pulled out a long brown strip.

Amigo sat down right away, licking his lips. He held perfectly still as Mr. Jackson balanced the treat on his nose. His eyes were very serious, as if he were taking an important test. He sat with the treat poised on his nose for one, two, three, four, five seconds before Mr. Jackson said, "Attaboy, Amigo. Bon appétit!"

In a flash, Amigo flipped the jerky into the air with his nose and caught it in his mouth.

"What a smart boy!" exclaimed the customer in line behind them. It was the young woman who'd been looking at the horse bridles. "Did you teach him that trick?" she asked.

"Yes," said Abby. "He can shake hands too. But those are just his party tricks. He's mostly trained as a service dog, but he's retired now. When he's working, people aren't supposed to pet him or pay attention to him. You can ask him to shake hands if you like."

The woman bent down and offered her hand to Amigo. He perked up his ears and lifted his paw for her.

"He says it's nice to meet you," said Abby.

"Oh, I've met Amigo before," said the woman. "Don't you remember?"

Abby searched her memory, feeling her face heat up with embarrassment. She often had trouble recognizing people when she saw them outside their

usual environment. She had even forgotten who Mr. Timothy was when she'd run into him at the zoo, and she saw him almost every day!

Abby glanced at the black leather bridle in the woman's hands. It was an English bridle, and she was wearing English riding boots. Emily and Grace rode English . . .

"Oh, you're my sisters' riding instructor," she said, connecting the dots. "I'm sorry, I forgot your name."

Abby had been to watch her sisters' riding lessons several times before. She remembered a farm with hilly pastures and multicolored jumps in the arena, but mostly she remembered the big, friendly gray-and-white English sheepdog that lived there.

"That's okay," said the woman. "It's Bonnie—Bonnie Summers."

"And your dog is named Shep," said Abby. "I'm better at remembering dogs than people."

Bonnie laughed. "I'm a lot better at remembering my students' horses names too. Grace has learned not to be offended if I call her Joker." That was the name of Grace's pony.

Mr. Jackson put the rabbit food into a plastic bag and gave it to Abby.

"See you later, Abby. Bye, Amigo!" said Bonnie, waving to them as they left the store.

Walking down Main Street, Abby spotted Mr.

Clark, an elderly man who had adopted a puppy from Second Chance Ranch a few months ago.

"Cinnamon's getting so big," said Abby, looking down at the reddish-brown cocker spaniel. Cinnamon looked back at her with soulful eyes, wagging her stumpy tail. She stood up and walked over to greet Amigo. Or, more accurately, she waddled.

"Actually, she looks a little bit fat, Mr. Clark," said Abby. "Have you been overfeeding her?"

Mr. Clark threw back his head and laughed. "Guilty as charged," he said. "She just gives me this certain look, and I can't say no. Who could resist those eyes?"

He had a point. "You should still try, though," said Abby. "She'll be healthier—and happier, too—if she loses some weight."

"My doctor tries to tell me the same thing," said Mr. Clark. "But I hear you. From now on, she only gets *one* sausage patty for breakfast."

No amount of sausage patties were really good for Cinnamon, but Abby noticed that Amigo was getting tired. He was lying down at her feet, which he didn't usually do while they were out. Abby decided to save her lecture on an appropriate canine diet for later.

As Abby and Amigo were walking down the winding country road to the ranch, they passed Mr. Alvarez in his mail truck. He stopped to chat too.

Mr. Alvarez always carried dog biscuits in his

pockets for the dogs along his route. He offered one to Amigo. But Amigo only sniffed it and turned his head away.

"He must be full from the jerky that Mr. Jackson gave him," Abby explained. She remembered that Amigo hadn't wanted his biscuits a few days ago, either. Maybe he didn't like them anymore. Once, Abby had eaten chicken nuggets for lunch every day for a month straight. Then, one day, she could hardly stand the sight of them.

When they finally got home, Amigo went straight to his bed in the living room and circled three times before he flopped down. Within minutes, he was asleep and snoring.

I hope the walk to town didn't wear him out too much, Abby worried. She hadn't expected to run into so many people they knew.

But Amigo seemed to have friends wherever he went. The thought made Abby smile. She couldn't imagine having to talk to all those people without Amigo by her side. They probably wouldn't even have stopped to notice her. But everyone noticed Amigo, and everyone loved him—just not as much as Abby did.

Chapter Five

"Breakfast, Amigo!" called Abby, forcing her voice to sound cheerful. She held her breath as she set the dish of moistened kibble and canned food on the floor in front of him.

For the past week, Amigo had hardly touched his breakfast or dinner. His coat was starting to look dull, and his body was thinner.

"He's still not eating?" asked her dad, frowning down at Amigo's full dish as he piled the breakfast dishes into the sink.

"He ate some of his dinner yesterday," said Abby. *After I topped it with peanut butter*, she added to herself.

"Hurry up, Abby, the bus is here!" cried Emily, swinging her backpack over her shoulder. Grace had already bolted out of the house. She'd been avoiding Abby as much as possible since their fight about the colored pencils, and that was just fine with Abby.

Abby reluctantly followed Emily outside, glancing back at Amigo. If only he could come to school with her. She'd be able to keep a closer eye on him, and the day ahead wouldn't seem as long.

Near the front of the bus, she spotted Cora, Cat,

and Savannah all crammed into one row of seats, even though each row was only meant to hold two people.

When the three of them saw Abby, they put their heads close together and whispered for a moment. Then Cora called out, "Come sit with us, Abby."

She moved across the aisle and patted the seat next to her.

Abby looked at them, then back at the seat at the back of the bus where she usually sat to be near Miriam. She didn't know what to do. She wanted to sit in both places at once.

"Hey, why did the chicken cross the road?" said Jamal's voice a few rows down. "Answer: It never did, because its name was Abby," he continued. "It just stood there, getting in everyone's way."

Abby made a face at Jamal, then turned her attention back to Cora. Everyone was looking at her expectantly, even all the other kids who had nothing to do with the situation.

"I sit with Miriam on the bus," Abby said finally to Cora. "But maybe we can hang out later." She practically ran past them down the aisle, nearly tripping on her shoelaces. She'd been in such a hurry to get out the door that she'd forgotten to tie them.

Abby settled into her usual seat, and Emily and Grace sat in one in front of her. Miriam got on at the next stop. She smiled as the wheelchair lift raised her onto the bus when she saw that Abby was in her usual seat.

Once the bus had started again, Miriam took out her phone and showed Abby some pictures from her visit to her grandmother's house. "This is the challah I made for the dinner after the Yom Kippur fast," she said, scrolling to a photo of a braided loaf of bread. "We were so hungry, there weren't even any leftovers for French toast the next morning."

"Hey, you're not wearing your new glasses," Abby noticed.

"Oh, right, those. I, um, convinced my parents to let me get contact lenses instead." Miriam's cheeks were a little flushed. "So, how was school while I was gone? Did I miss anything important?"

"No, just terrariums," said Abby. "And my plumeria seed didn't sprout, unfortunately. I think the classroom is too cold. How's Destiny?"

"She was glad to see me when I went to visit Caleb yesterday," said Miriam. "He spoils her so much, though. He lets her sleep on the couch, and I know he feeds her table scraps, because she kept begging for my popcorn."

Abby felt a lump form in her throat as she remembered Amigo staring listlessly at his breakfast that morning.

"Abby, is something wrong?" asked Miriam.

"Amigo had a . . . another problem with his heart," said Abby, fussing with the zipper on her backpack.

"Oh no! Is he okay now?"

"Yes," said Abby. "He's much better. I just have to be careful not to overexcite him. He can't play with Bella or the other rescue dogs anymore."

Miriam nodded. "You take such great care of him, I'm sure he'll be back to his old self in no time."

🐾

That afternoon, Abby came home to find both her parents sitting at the kitchen table. Cups of tea rested in front of them, like they'd been there awhile.

That was unusual. Usually, her mom was still at the animal hospital when Abby got home from school and her dad was outside attending to the ranch.

Abby said hi to her parents and started to head past them to find Amigo.

"Abby," said Mr. Ramirez. "Can you sit down for a minute? We need to talk to you."

"Grace, Emily," Mrs. Ramirez said to the girls, who had followed Abby into the kitchen. "Will you give us a moment with Abby, please?"

"Sure, Mom," Emily said, pulling Grace's arm into the living room before she could protest. "We'll go upstairs."

Abby felt her heart start beating fast, although

she didn't know why. Instead of sitting down, she stood frozen.

"It's about Amigo," said Mrs. Ramirez gently. "Sweetie, you know he hasn't been eating well for the last few weeks. He's starting to lose weight and become malnourished."

"He doesn't have to eat dog food," said Abby, her voice rising high. "He likes peanut butter sandwiches. He can eat those instead."

"Abby," said Mrs. Ramirez, in a still gentle, but firmer voice. "Amigo is suffering. Not eating is his way of telling us that he's in pain and not enjoying his life."

"That's not true!" Abby turned and went into the living room. Her parents got up to follow her. Amigo was lying in his fleecy bed. Abby went over to him and stroked the softest fur on the side of his muzzle, where the whiskers sprouted. "Amigo loves me."

"Yes, Amigo loves you," said Mr. Ramirez. "And we know how much you love him. That's why you have to think about what's best for him right now."

Abby rested her hand on Amigo's side. His heart was beating in an even rhythm under her hands. She could feel each of his ribs. She could see the gray hairs that had spread across his face, the color fading from his nose and now from around his eyes.

"You've helped take care of a lot of animals at the ranch," said Mr. Ramirez. "You've been able to help dogs that nobody else could help. And when animals have come here that are too sick for us to help, you've comforted them at the end of their lives. You've been strong and brave for animals facing a lot of pain."

Abby felt like her own heart had stopped beating. "You want to put Amigo to sleep," she said, staring at her parents as if they were strangers. "You want to kill him."

"The first promise that veterinarians make is to do no harm to animals," said Mrs. Ramirez. "That includes not letting them suffer unnecessarily. I know it's really hard to think about, but . . ."

Her mother kept speaking, but Abby couldn't hear her. She looked wildly around the room. She felt like an animal trapped in a cage.

For some reason, her eyes fixed on a glass statue on a shelf next to the living room couch. It was in the shape of two wild horses galloping together, their flowing manes and tales intertwined. It had been a wedding gift to her parents from Abby's abuela, who had died a few years ago.

Before she even realized what she was doing, Abby darted across the room and climbed up on the arm of the couch. She grabbed the statue from the shelf and held it high in the air above her head.

Time seemed to freeze for a moment. She saw her parents' startled expressions and Amigo curled in his basket near the window, his eyes already drooping closed again.

"This is how I feel about what you're telling me!" Abby yelled.

She threw the statue down as hard as she could. It hit the floor and exploded into thousands of glittering shards.

Abby jumped off the arm of the couch, launching herself across the mess of broken glass. She ran past her parents, whose faces were still frozen in shock. She grabbed Amigo by his collar and hurried him up the stairs to her room, slamming the door behind her.

Abby zipped Amigo into the Cave of Solitude with her and held him tightly, whispering out loud that she would never, ever let anyone take him away from her.

🐾

It was after midnight. Abby lay awake in bed, listening for any sound in the silent house. She reached down and put her hand on Amigo's head, reassuring herself that he was still there.

After Abby had run up to her room, she'd heard the low murmur of her parents' voices for a while, followed by the tinkle of broken glass being swept up. A little while later, Mrs. Ramirez had come up to Abby's room.

"Am I in trouble about the statue?" Abby had asked from inside her Cave of Solitude, with Amigo.

She'd heard her mother's sigh, even though she couldn't see her. "That statue was very special to your dad and me," her mom said. "It's not something that can be replaced. But I know you're much more upset about Amigo than I am about the statue. Your dad and I feel the same way. Amigo isn't just a pet, he's a member of our family."

Then her mother had said Abby should get some rest and they would talk about it more in the morning.

But Abby wouldn't be there in the morning, and neither would Amigo. A few hours later, Abby rolled out of bed and led Amigo into the hall and down the creaky stairs as quietly as possible.

She froze as someone stirred and muttered in Grace and Emily's room. She waited for a minute, hardly breathing, and then continued down the stairs.

In the mudroom, Abby grabbed her school backpack and took out all her books and homework. She went to the kitchen to fill a thermos with water and threw a box of granola bars, a jar of peanut butter, and Amigo's bottles of medicine into the backpack. She grabbed a polar-fleece blanket from the living room and a flashlight from the junk drawer, and stuffed those into the backpack too.

Abby clipped a leash to Amigo's collar. She opened the mudroom door as quietly as she could and led him through it. They crossed the semicircle of lawn lit by the farmhouse's porch light.

Abby clutched Amigo's leash tighter as they reached the edge of the warm yellow light. She took a deep breath and another step. The night swept in to fill her eyes and ears like a wave breaking over her head.

Chapter Six

Abby opened the gate to the horse pasture behind the barn and led Amigo through it. A breeze swept across the grassy expanse, and Abby shivered. The autumn days were still hot in central Texas, but the nights could get close to freezing. Abby wasn't used to being outside at night, and she hadn't thought to bring a jacket. She thought about going to get one, but she couldn't risk her family waking up.

Turning back at the far end of the pasture, she could just make out the shape of the white ranch house on the hill. Fumbling in her backpack, Abby took out her flashlight and switched it on. She didn't have to worry about anyone seeing her now. The area behind the ranch was acres of wilderness, of scrubland and forest.

She didn't really have a plan. Her only thought was to get as far away from the ranch as possible. Her parents might know a lot about animals, but they were wrong about Amigo. If they were going to try to take him away, she'd just have to go where they couldn't find her.

Amigo looked back toward the ranch and let out a worried bark. Abby shushed him, and Amigo looked up at her. He nudged his nose against her hand. It was his signal to her that she might be getting upset and should take a deep breath.

"It's okay, Amigo," Abby said. "I don't need your help now. I'm doing this for you."

She tugged on Amigo's leash to get him moving, and a plan started to form in her mind. Last summer, her family had spent a weekend at a campsite in the wilderness area, about an hour's hike from the ranch.

Abby had a good memory for places. If she'd been somewhere once, she could usually remember how to get back there again. But could she find the campsite in the dark?

Patchy clouds covered the sky. When the moon shone down, the landscape was almost as bright as in the daylight. But when a cloud rolled across the moon, Abby could barely see two steps in front of her. She moved the beam of her flashlight around as she walked, searching out familiar landmarks.

She had to shift between looking at the horizon and at her feet. Clumps of sagebrush and mesquite seedlings sprouted from the sandy soil, tall enough to trip her. She paused often, both to get her bearings and to let Amigo rest.

A few black shapes swooped silently across the sky. Abby wondered what kind of birds they were, then realized they were bats. She reminded herself that bats used echolocation to catch mosquitos and other insects that could transmit diseases to livestock. They were friends.

After fifteen minutes, she spotted a rock formation shaped kind of like a sheep. Her family called it "Buck Rock." Twenty minutes later, she saw a wooden birdhouse that Emily and their dad had set up as a nesting site for endangered golden-cheeked warblers. She was getting close now.

At last, she reached the familiar clearing where her family had camped. Sagebrush and boulders surrounded one side, and a sparse forest of pine and juniper trees on the other. A wooden picnic table sat in the center of the clearing. Next to it was a fire pit ringed with stones and covered with a metal grate for grilling.

On the ground near the campfire, Abby spotted the Dallas Cowboys cap that Grace had complained about losing for weeks. These small signs of civilization made Abby feel a little less anxious about being outside in the woods in the middle of the night.

At the edge of the clearing was a large tree with a wide, smooth trunk. Abby remembered sitting beneath it, reading, while her dad grilled hot dogs and her sisters argued about the right way to set up the tent.

Abby set her backpack on the ground and spread the polar-fleece blanket out beneath the tree. She sat down with her back propped against the tree trunk. Amigo sank wearily down beside her.

The ground beneath the blanket felt hard and lumpy. Abby coaxed Amigo to his feet, then got up and folded the blanket into quarters. She laid it down again and patted it until Amigo settled back onto its soft, thick folds. It was too small for both of them now, but Abby didn't mind sitting on the ground.

Suddenly, Amigo let out a high-pitched whine, staring intently into a thick tangle of sagebrush at the edge of the clearing.

Abby stared into the darkness, and she noticed a pair of yellow eyes glowed back her. Abby felt a shudder of fear. What if it was a coyote—or worse? She looked at Amigo. His ears were alert, and the fur on the back of his neck was standing up.

Abby grabbed a rock from the ground and threw it at the pair of eyes. "Get lost!" she yelled.

She heard a rustling sound, and the eyes blinked away into the darkness. Abby watched for a long time, but they didn't come back. She felt her heart begin to beat slower and her tense muscles relax. Amigo rolled onto his side and started snoring gently. Abby slid over and lay down next to him. His body felt warm against hers in the chilly night.

An owl hooted in the branches of the pine tree above them. For some reason, the sound was comforting. Soon, in spite of the cold, rocky ground and

the rustling in the bushes around her, Abby drifted off to sleep.

🐾

Abby woke up the next morning to the sound of birdsong. Actually, it sounded like the birds were having a music festival. In the bright morning sunshine, the wilderness around her wasn't so frightening. Being out here seemed almost like an adventure.

Amigo was still curled up in a ball beside her, his tail tucked over his nose for warmth. He woke up, blinking sleepily, as she rummaged through her backpack.

Abby took out a granola bar for herself and opened the jar of peanut butter for Amigo. Getting to finish a nearly empty jar was usually one of his favorite treats. But he didn't want any today. She gave him his medicine anyway, pushing the pills into his mouth and then stroking his throat gently until he swallowed.

Abby drank some of the water in her thermos, and then poured the rest into her cupped hand. Amigo lapped it up gratefully.

The thermos was empty now, but Abby remembered that there was a stream somewhere nearby. She got up and strolled in the direction she thought it was. The trees created a lot of shade, and the grass was still cool and dewy. She heard the gurgle of water and followed the sound to a rocky spring that bubbled up from the ground.

She crouched down to fill up her thermos. She wouldn't drink the water, but she got it in case Amigo wanted more. The shallow water running over the rocks and sand looked so inviting that Abby took off her shoes and waded into it. The water was icy, but for some reason, Abby didn't mind. She giggled as minnows swarmed against the current toward her feet and pecked specks of silt from her bare toes. Whenever she took a step, she left a footprint that was quickly eroded by the water.

Abby was having so much fun that she decided to go back and get Amigo. Unlike some dogs, he liked playing in water. Maybe it was because he was a golden retriever, a breed that had been developed to hunt ducks and other waterfowl. At home, he'd grab his bottle of shampoo from the shelf and drop it into her lap whenever he thought it was time for a bath.

Abby waded over to the shore and slung her shoes over her shoulder by the laces as she headed back toward the campsite. Amigo lifted his head when she reached the clearing and whistled for him. But he didn't get up.

"Hey, Amigo!" she called out. "Want to go for a *swim*?"

But even that magic word didn't make Amigo

get to his feet. Abby looked closer and noticed his ribs heaving up and down. His breathing was fast and shallow, like he'd been running in the hot sun, even though he hadn't gotten up since last night. His head wobbled a little on his shoulders, as if it were too heavy for him to hold up.

Abby went over and knelt down on the ground in front of him. She stroked his soft ears and his forehead again and again, trying to smooth away the worry lines that had grown so deep on his forehead.

His tail fluttered softly against the ground, too weak to wag properly. He looked up at her, his eyes calm and trusting.

Something wet splashed onto Amigo's fur. Abby touched a hand to her face and felt tears streaming down it. She realized that her body already knew the truth before her mind was willing to accept it.

Even though Amigo had stopped wearing his service dog vest, he had never stopped looking out for Abby. Now he had reached the end of his life, and he was waiting for her to let him know that she would be okay without him.

Chapter Seven

"Abby! Abby!"

From somewhere far away, Abby heard familiar voices calling her name. But she didn't answer. She couldn't. She wanted her family with her, and at the same time, she never wanted to see them again. She just wanted time to stop so she could stay here with Amigo forever.

Footsteps rustled in the grass nearby. "There you are!" said a familiar voice.

Abby looked up and saw Grace standing at the edge of the clearing. Abby turned her face away and pressed it into Amigo's fur. Of everyone in her family, Grace was the last person Abby wanted to see. She was the last person who would understand.

"I thought this was where you'd be," said Grace. "I remembered how much you liked camping here."

Abby didn't say anything. She heard Grace pick up Abby's flashlight and click it on and off, then the sound of her rifling through the stuff in Abby's backpack.

"I ran away, too, when my mom was sick," Grace said finally.

That made Abby lift up her head. Grace hardly

ever talked about the time before she and Emily had come to live with the Ramirez family.

Grace sat cross-legged on the ground a little distance away. "Mom was already unconscious by then—in a coma, I guess," she said. "The chemotherapy had made her really weak, and sometimes, she didn't recognize me and Emily. Finally, our grandma made us both sit down. She told us that Mom probably wasn't ever going to wake up."

Grace paused. Abby saw her sister's face moving between sadness and anger. She waited until Grace continued.

"Until then, everyone had said that Mom was going to be okay. The doctors, the nurses, the neighbor who stayed with us . . . All of them were lying because they didn't want to scare us. Emily and I could see Mom getting sicker and sicker, but until then, nobody told us that she might die."

Grace stopped talking again. She picked up a pointy piece of rock and gouged it into the dirt.

"When Grandma told us, Emily started crying," she said. "But I just got up and ran. I ran away from the hospital and from what she was saying. I went and hid in an abandoned building near our apartment. I stayed there for two nights, and I wasn't smart enough to bring blankets and food like you were."

"Did someone come and find you?" asked Abby.

"No," said Grace. "They looked for me, but I'm really good at hiding. I went back because I didn't want Emily to be without me. And I realized that our mom was going to die whether I was there or not. I didn't want to miss the time I had left with her."

"Amigo's dying too," said Abby.

"I know," Grace said simply. "I'm sorry." Then she stood up. "I'll be back soon."

She left the clearing. Abby lost track of time as she rested her head on Amigo's chest, listening to the sound of his heartbeat. She could almost feel the minutes and the seconds slipping away.

Abby heard voices again and the sound of footsteps.

She felt, rather than heard or saw, her family settling down around her. Her mom knelt beside Amigo and rested her hand on top of Abby's. Abby opened her blurry eyes and saw her dad next to her mom, with his arm around her shoulder. Grace leaned up against him, with Emily beside her.

Natalie knelt down next to Abby. She slipped her hand into Abby's and held it. Emily took Natalie's other hand. Soon, the whole family sat in a circle, joined by Amigo.

"I remember the day Amigo came home," said Natalie, breaking the heavy silence that had settled over the clearing. Even the birds had gone quiet. "Abby still didn't talk then. But as we were all getting

out of the car, she pointed to the house and said, 'Amigo lives here.' "

"And I remember the first day that Amigo went to school with Abby," said their mom. "By the time she came home that afternoon, she'd already made a new friend—Miriam."

"Thank you, Amigo, for being a true friend to Abby and to all of us," said their dad.

"Thank you, Amigo," Emily echoed softly.

"Goodbye, Amigo," said Grace.

Abby couldn't say anything. She didn't need to. Amigo understood. He lifted his head and licked Abby's hand. Then he lay still on the blanket and let out a long, deep sigh.

He didn't take another breath.

Abby bowed her head and squeezed Natalie's hand as tightly as she could.

Amigo, Amigo . . . She remembered how that first word had felt, bursting out of her mouth like a blade of grass from thawed ground in the spring. Now, once again, it felt like the only word Abby could remember, the only word she knew.

Amigo . . .

Chapter Eight

Mrs. Ramirez knocked softly on the door to Abby's room. "Everyone's here, if you're ready to come down now."

It was Saturday, two days after Amigo had died. Mr. Ramirez had brought Amigo's body back from the campsite and buried it next to the oak tree in the yard where Amigo liked to lie in the shade. His grave marker was a smooth, round stone of white quartz.

Today was his memorial service. It had been Natalie's idea, and she had been in charge of inviting everyone.

Abby climbed reluctantly out of her Cave of Solitude, where she'd been reading her science class textbook. She hadn't been back to school since she'd run away and Amigo had died. Even though she didn't feel very interested in the photosynthesis cycle just then, it was practically the only book in her room that wasn't about dogs, and she had schoolwork to catch up on.

Abby didn't want to read about dogs. She didn't want to think about them. She didn't really want to think about anything, because every thought seemed to remind her that Amigo was gone.

But now, people were downstairs, waiting for her.

In the kitchen, the counter was packed with food in covered dishes. The table was scattered with framed pictures of Amigo, which Natalie or someone must have collected from all over the house.

Abby went out into the yard and was surprised to see how many people were gathered. Her parents, her sisters, and a big group of her aunts and uncles and cousins were there. And there were Marco and his dad, Natalie's friend Darcy and her mom, Mr. Jackson, Mr. Alvarez, Mr. Clark, and at least a dozen other people Abby had helped choose dogs for.

She felt almost dizzy as she stared out at the sea of faces. She saw Mr. Timothy, LeeAnn, her school principal, Mrs. Jeffrey, and at least half the students from her fifth-grade class. Cora, Cat, and Savannah weren't there, but to Abby's surprise, Jamal was.

"Everyone, can I have your attention, please," said Natalie in her most grown-up voice. She was standing by the oak tree, near the white stone that marked Amigo's grave. She motioned for Abby to join her.

Abby went reluctantly to stand next to her sister and kept her eyes fixed on the ground.

"It means so much to our family that everyone gathered with us today to celebrate Amigo's life," said Natalie, her voice carrying across the yard. "Amigo wasn't just Abby's companion and service dog, but he was also a member of the community. I remem- ber when Second Chance Ranch had a booth at the

Sugarberry Fair a few years ago. Everyone wanted to adopt Amigo the second they saw him, but of course, he wasn't one of our rescue dogs. A lot of people were really disappointed. Then Abby came up with the idea to raffle off a 'date' with Amigo, where the winner could take him for a walk and play games with him for the whole afternoon. We had a lot of fun dressing him up in a doggy tux and making a silly video showing him and Abby strolling in the park and sharing an ice cream cone. We thought it was just a fun idea that might raise a few dollars for the ranch, but it ended up raising more than five hundred dollars. Abby was so generous to let someone share Amigo for that day, and that wasn't the only time Amigo made a difference . . ."

Natalie went on to tell more stories. When she had finished, other people shared memories about Amigo too. Abby was surprised by how many people spoke. Even people who had only met him a few times remembered him.

"Do you want to say anything, Abby?" Natalie whispered to her.

For a moment, Abby wished she were like Natalie. She wished she could stand in front of all these people and come up with just the right thing to say. But her feelings were deeper than anything she could put into a speech. She shook her head. Natalie gave her shoulder a little squeeze. She knew that Abby didn't always express herself in words.

Natalie said a few more things and invited everyone to stay for lunch. She went inside to help in the kitchen, leaving Abby standing in the yard.

A phrase that Natalie had used kept repeating in Abby's mind: *"Amigo might be gone, but he's still with us in our hearts."* What did that even mean? Blood was in Abby's heart, and Amigo was buried in the ground, where his body would slowly turn back into elements like carbon and phosphorous that would help the grass grow.

One by one, all the people in the yard came up to Abby to tell her how sorry they were about Amigo. Soon, Abby's head began to ache. She was tired of saying, "Thank you for coming today." She didn't want to talk about how sad she was, and she didn't know what else to say. She had no idea how some people—most people—seemed to just magically know what to say in different situations.

"Amigo was a great friend," said Mr. Timothy when he came over to greet her, along with the students from the class. He handed her a card that everyone had signed.

"I'm sorry about Amigo," said Jamal. "He was a cool dog, and I liked playing ball with him when he wasn't on the job."

Sometimes at recess, Abby had taken off Amigo's

service dog vest and let him take a break to run around with everyone. Even though he was a dog, he'd been practically the most popular kid in the class.

Abby spotted Miriam and Caleb a little distance away. Caleb had brought Destiny too.

"Oh, Abby, I'm so sorry for your loss," said Miriam as they came closer. Destiny nudged Abby with her pointy nose, and Abby patted her head automatically. Her fur was different than Amigo's, shorter and coarser.

Abby thanked Miriam, like she had thanked everyone else. Her head was spinning from the sound of so many conversations around her, so many people talking about Amigo.

"I brought you this poem," said Miriam. She wheeled a little closer and held out a framed picture she had been holding in her lap.

Abby took it and stared down at it. The background was a photo of a sky covered by a rainbow. The text was printed on top of it. The poem was about some animals that had died crossing over a rainbow bridge in the sky.

A strange, hot feeling swept over Abby as she read it. She felt her jaw clench up and her throat sting.

"That's ridiculous," she said. "Rainbows are made out of droplets of water in the atmosphere that refract light. Animals, or anybody, can't cross them. They'd fall through the air and die."

Miriam's eyes widened. "I'm sorry," she whispered. "I thought it might make you feel better."

Before Abby could reply, she felt a hand on her shoulder and heard someone saying her name. She spun around and saw her mom standing next to Chris, the trainer from the Helping Paws Center where Abby had gotten Amigo.

"Excuse me for interrupting your conversation, but Chris can't stay long," said Mrs. Ramirez. "He's on his way to bring a family their new guide dog. I wanted to make sure you got a chance to talk to him before he had to leave."

"Abby, I'm so sorry about Amigo," said Chris. "He was one of a kind."

"Yes," said Abby. Amigo's training had been finished years ago, but Abby still brought him to the Helping Paws Center to visit sometimes. Whenever she saw Chris, she always asked him to tell the story of Amigo meeting her for the first time, after Amigo's old owners had returned him to the center.

Chris always said, "Truth is, you both seemed so sad the first time you walked through that door. But by the time you left together, you were smiling and Amigo's tail was wagging so fast, I was afraid he'd wear it out and need a new one."

The way Chris said it always made Abby laugh. But she didn't want to hear that story today.

Chris said he had to go anyway. He told Abby that

her parents had made a contribution to the Helping Paws Center in Amigo's memory. Grace and Emily had given their allowances too.

When Chris left, Abby turned back around and saw that Miriam and Caleb were gone. One by one, the other guests left too. The stone that marked Amigo's grave was now covered with flowers, photos, and stuffed toys. Abby put the framed poem that Miriam had given her with it. She wished she could unsay what she'd said about it.

But time only goes in one direction. She could almost reach out and touch her memories of a time when there was nothing next to the oak tree except grass. Or even Amigo himself, panting happily as he rested in the dappled shade.

Abby squeezed her eyes shut and tried to will the memory to become real. She focused on every detail, from the exact golden shade of his fur to the lavender scent of the special dog shampoo she used for his weekly bath.

But when she opened her eyes, the only thing in front of her was the white stone, the flowers and gifts, and no Amigo.

He was only alive in Abby's memories now. For as long as she lived, Amigo would be there, filling almost every moment she could remember.

Chapter Nine

Abby sat on the green couch in LeeAnn's office. LeeAnn was in the tan chair nearby. She sat with her hands folded over one knee, waiting until Abby was ready to speak.

On a low wooden table between them was a box of tissues, a rubber stress ball filled with plastic beads, and a box of laminated cards with the names of different emotions on them.

Abby picked up the stack of cards and flipped through it. Happy. Excited. Relieved. Playful . . . Definitely not.

Sad. Upset. Worried. Angry . . . Closer, but none of them felt quite right.

"It's like sad, but different," said Abby, looking up from the cards. Abby didn't usually like to look people in the eye, but LeeAnn's eyes were calm and still, like a clear sky. They rarely changed or held messages that Abby didn't understand.

"Where do you feel it in your body?" asked LeeAnn.

Abby put a hand on the center of her chest, spreading her fingers out. "Here . . ."

"I think the word you might be thinking of is *grief*," said LeeAnn. "It's different than regular sadness. It means you lost someone or something that you loved very much. You might spend a lot of time thinking about the past. You might even remember all the joy and happiness that Amigo brought you and feel like there's an emptiness in your life now that he's gone."

"I used to have a lot of time on my activities chart just for Amigo," said Abby. "I could put other things in for those times, but I don't want to. I just want to leave them blank."

Actually, she thought, *I want Amigo to be here.* But that wasn't possible, so she didn't say it out loud.

"At Amigo's memorial service, Miriam gave me a poem about the Rainbow Bridge," she told LeeAnn instead. "I told her it was stupid, and then she left. I sat by myself on the bus today."

"It's normal to get angry when you're grieving," said LeeAnn. "Miriam's feelings might have been hurt, but I think she probably understands."

"Other than Amigo, Miriam is probably my only friend," said Abby. "For a while, I thought that Cora, Cat, and Savannah were, but now I know they were just faking."

She traced her fingers around the edges of the cards in her hands. "One is 50 percent of two, but it seems like less. Almost like zero. Miriam really likes dogs, and now I don't like to talk about dogs anymore."

"Do you ever talk about other things with Miriam?"

"Sometimes. But mostly dogs."

Abby set down the flashcards and picked up the stress ball. She squeezed it, feeling the beads inside shift beneath her fingers. She tossed it back and forth from hand to hand.

"It's almost time to end our session for today," said LeeAnn. "But remember, you can come and talk to me any time. And, Abby?"

"Yes?"

"I think you have more than one friend."

"Why do you think that?" Abby asked.

"How many people came to Amigo's memorial service?" asked LeeAnn. "About fifty?"

"Fifty-four," said Abby. "Fifty-five if you count Destiny. But they were Amigo's friends, not mine."

"Memorial services are for people who are still alive, Abby. They came to see you."

❖

"Wait a minute, Abby, I want to show you something," said Mr. Timothy after class that day. As the other students streamed out of the classroom, she followed him over to the row of terrariums by the window. In hers, Abby was surprised to see something in the corner that had remained bare for the past few weeks.

"The plumeria!" said Abby, leaning down to look

at the slender green shoot. "I didn't think it would grow." So far, it looked nothing like the beautiful star-shaped flower on the seed packet, but it was definitely sprouting.

"Plants are surprisingly resilient," said Mr. Timothy. "They often find ways to survive, even in less-than-ideal conditions."

Abby felt a little better as she left the classroom. But she was still too anxious to sit with Miriam on the bus ride home. She waited on purpose until the bus was almost full and then slipped into the seat behind Ms. Bea that was always empty.

She was afraid to find out if LeeAnn was right or if she had lost Miriam's friendship forever.

🐾

"Ouch!" cried Abby. She dropped the slinky brown ferret back into its cage. The ferret scuttled away into a plastic Critter Trail tunnel.

"She bit me," said Abby, examining a row of pink dots on the back of her hand.

Emily looked up from the pair of white rats she was playing with. One of them was sitting on her shoulder, and the other peeked out of the sleeve of her sweatshirt.

"Ferrets don't like to be picked up like that," said Emily. "She probably thought you were a predator trying to eat her. If you need to handle her, it's better to grab her by the loose skin at the back of her neck and support her feet."

"Oh," said Abby. She crouched down to peer into the plastic tubes of the Critter Trail. The ferret looked back at her with beady black eyes, then turned and retreated deeper into its hiding place.

Abby sighed. Now that Amigo was gone, Abby didn't want to work with the dogs on the ranch anymore. She'd thought that switching tasks with Grace would make things easier.

Grace had agreed to take over the dog chores. In exchange, Abby had to help Emily take care of all the small animals, plus feed Grace's purebred Persian cat, Chances, and muck out Joker's stall.

The ferret didn't seem to be in a very playful mood, but maybe she'd have better luck with Chances. Abby left Emily in the small-animal room and headed to the pantry to grab a can of cat food.

She opened it and dumped the cylinder of seafood pâté into Chances's dish, mushing it around with a fork to break it into pieces. Then she covered the dish with a paper towel and put it in the microwave for fifteen seconds.

Grace had insisted that because Chances was so aristocratic, she would only eat food that had been warmed up to the temperature of a freshly caught mouse. Abby had snorted at that. She was pretty sure that lazy, spoiled Chances had never caught a mouse in her life. She couldn't imagine a dog ever being that fussy.

"Chances!" Abby called, setting the mouse-temperature food on the floor. "Dinnertime!"

But Chances was nowhere to be found. Abby remembered what Grace had told her: "Make sure she eats her food while it's still fresh. She won't touch it once it starts to dry out."

"Chances!" Abby yelled again. Nothing. Well, if Chances wasn't going to show up, Abby would just have to find her. She traipsed upstairs to Grace and Emily's room. Chances liked to sleep on Grace's bed— or better yet, in the laundry basket filled with clean clothes that Grace rarely remembered to fold and put away.

Chances wasn't on the bed, and she wasn't in the laundry basket. She also wasn't in any of the other bedrooms, under the couch in the living room, behind the towels in the bathroom closet, with the rescued cats in the cat room, or curled up on the pile of jackets in the mudroom. She hadn't snuck into the small-animal room, and she definitely wasn't in the dog kennel.

At last, Abby ran out of hiding places. Was it possible Chances had sneaked out of the house somehow? Abby had accidentally left the door ajar earlier when she went outside. If Chances had gotten lost, Grace would never forgive Abby.

Abby walked back into the kitchen, completing her full circle of the house. Her mind raced as she thought of how to break the news to Grace.

Then she did a double take as she spotted something white and fluffy on the floor near the refrigerator. There was Chances, crouched in front of her food dish, munching away. When she saw Abby, she swished her puffy tail across the floor and let out a cranky meow.

"I'm not sure I understand what Grace sees in you," Abby remarked. To her, Chances looked like a feather duster and had about as much personality.

Leaving Chances to finish dining in peace, Abby headed out to the barn to clean Joker's stall. Crossing the yard, she noticed Grace taking Bella for a run in the back pasture.

Bella galloped ahead of Grace, pulling on the leash and dragging her from one interesting smell to the next. Bella's jet-black fur was glossy in the sun. Every movement she made seemed to be an overflow of joyful energy.

Abby felt a pang of regret. If only she were out there playing with Bella instead. But no—how could Abby have fun with another dog? It would be like saying Amigo didn't matter, that she had replaced him.

Abby looked away and continued trudging toward the barn.

"Oh, good," said Natalie when Abby walked in. "Joker's stall is a real mess today. Be sure to use the *big* wheelbarrow. But before you get started, help me scrub these water buckets. Honestly, I have no idea how they get so slimy."

Chapter Ten

The phone rang, startling Abby as she loaded the dishwasher full of crusty cat food dishes. Dog dishes were easier to clean because the dogs usually licked their bowls until they sparkled.

The phone rang a second time, but Abby ignored it. Usually, one of her parents or Natalie picked up the phone. There was an extension out in the barn.

The phone was still ringing. Abby picked it up. "Hello, Second Chance Ranch," she said. "This is Abby speaking."

"Hi, Abby. It's Chris from the Helping Paws Center," said the familiar deep voice on the other end of the line. "How are you?"

"Hi," said Abby. "I'm okay." It wasn't exactly true, but it was easier than trying to describe how she really was. "I don't think my parents are around right now. Would you like me to take a message?"

"I actually called to talk to you," said Chris. "I wanted to ask your advice about something."

"Really?" asked Abby. Chris was a professional dog trainer. She couldn't imagine why he would need her advice about anything.

"A family contacted me recently," said Chris. "They're looking for a service dog for their son who has autism. But I don't have any available right now. The two dogs that I have in training are both guide dogs for the blind. But I told them I might be able to help them find a suitable dog to train, if they're willing to wait. I was wondering if there are any dogs at Second Chance Ranch that might be good candidates."

Abby thought about it. Not just any dog would make a good service animal. In the past month, two new dogs had come to the ranch. One was a Chihuahua named Polly. She had been treated badly by her last owner, and sometimes, she bit people because she was afraid.

The other new arrival was a border collie named Sloan. He was smart, but he needed to spend a lot of time outside, ideally herding animals. A service dog needed to stay close to its owner most of the time.

Then Abby thought of Bella. She was still pretty young for service dog training, but she was smart and friendly. Abby remembered how she had settled down by Amigo's side and comforted him when he was sick.

"There is one," she said. "A black Labrador named Bella."

"That's great," Chris said enthusiastically. "Could I set up a time to come meet her?"

"Sure," said Abby. "When?"

"How about tomorrow afternoon, around four o'clock?"

"Okay." Abby marked it down on the calendar next to the phone.

"I'll see you and Bella tomorrow, then," said Chris.

"Oh, it won't be me," said Abby. "I don't work with the dogs anymore. Grace does that. She can introduce you to Bella."

"No more dogs?" asked Chris, sounding surprised. "That doesn't seem like the Abby I know."

That's because I'm not the same Abby anymore.

To Chris, she said, "I work mostly with the small animals now. Right now, we have three rabbits, a ferret, two rats, and a chinchilla. But I don't think any of them would make good service animals."

"No," said Chris. "Dogs are usually the best. Although I did train a miniature horse once."

"I'll let Grace know you're coming tomorrow," said Abby.

"Okay," said Chris. "Thanks, Abby."

"Goodbye."

After she hung up the phone, Abby went and found Grace out in the yard with Bella. She told her about Chris's visit.

"Awesome," said Grace. "Although I kind of hope Bella doesn't have to leave the ranch soon. She's so much fun!"

Bella was jumping up and down, waiting for Grace to throw the Frisbee in her hand. She leaped up and put her paws on Grace's chest.

Grace laughed and grabbed Bella's paws, hopping up and down with Bella like they were two kangaroos.

"You shouldn't let her do that," said Abby with a frown. "It's bad manners."

"I know, but it's so funny," said Grace. She sent the Frisbee whizzing across the yard, and Bella raced after it.

"Chris is going to want to see if Bella has the right temperament for a service dog. That means she needs to be calm and obedient when he visits. And she needs to not jump on people. You should also work on her sit-stay commands."

Grace sighed. "Okay," she said. "Can you show me how?"

Abby hesitated. Just seeing Bella playing in the yard made her remember the day Amigo had collapsed. "I can lend you a book about dog training," she said.

"A book?" Grace complained. "You know I'm not really into books."

"Okay, then I'll send you a link to some videos online," said Abby. Bella trotted up to her and dropped the Frisbee at her feet. She looked up at Abby and let out an eager bark.

The sound sent a sharp pain through Abby's heart. She took a step back from Bella, then turned and hurried away into the house. Amigo had been Abby's dog, her only dog, and he was gone now.

Grace would just have to do her best with Bella on her own.

🐾

The next day, Abby lingered outside to the kennel room, sweeping the hallway just in front of the half-open door. She wasn't eavesdropping, exactly . . . She just happened to be able to hear and see what was going on inside.

What she heard was the sound of Bella's nails tapping in an excited rhythm on the wooden floor. What she saw was Bella leaping up and trying to lick Chris's face.

"Oops, sorry!" said Grace, grabbing Bella by the collar and pulling her away. "Sit, Bella."

Bella jumped up and tried to lick Grace's face instead.

"Um, we're still working on 'sit' and 'stay,' but she's the best ever at fetching," said Grace. Abby heard the squeak of a rubber toy, then saw Bella hurtle past the doorway toward the far end of the kennel.

In her enthusiasm, Bella went sailing right past the toy and crashed into an empty dog crate. But she quickly regained her footing and seized the squeaky toy in her jaws. She returned to drop it at Grace's feet, doing a happy dance around her.

"I can see that Bella really likes to play," said Chris. "Does she know how to walk on a leash?"

"Oh, totally!" said Grace.

A minute later, Grace was apologizing to Chris again as she unwrapped Bella's twisted leash from around his ankles.

"Do you want to see her flying Frisbee catch?"

asked Grace. "She gets so much air, just like the dogs on Animal Planet."

"I think I've seen enough for today," said Chris. "Thanks so much for letting me meet her."

Grace put Bella outside in the dog run, then she and Chris headed toward the doorway. Abby hurried away from the door, pretending that she had been sweeping farther down the hall.

"I have my riding lesson now," said Grace as they stepped out into the hall. "See you later, Chris!" She dashed away, presumably to find Emily.

Chris waved goodbye to her, then turned to Abby. "I think Bella has potential as a service dog," he said, even though Abby hadn't asked him anything. "She's friendly, intelligent, and very focused on people."

Abby couldn't help it . . . She felt a thrill of excitement and pride at the thought of Bella becoming a service dog.

"But she needs a lot of work," Chris added. "Right now, she doesn't even know basic obedience. She would also need a lot of specialized training to work with somebody who has autism."

Abby nodded. Amigo had known so many different commands. She knew it had taken years to train him.

"What do you think?" asked Chris. "Are you up for the challenge?"

Abby nearly dropped the broom she was holding. "Grace works with the dogs now," she reminded him.

"I'm sure that Grace takes great care of Bella and the other dogs," said Chris, "but she doesn't have the patience and experience that you do."

That was true. Bella obviously adored Grace, just like she adored everyone, but she didn't really *listen* to Grace. Abby could help Bella learn to obey her handler while still having fun.

"Grace has also never had a service dog before, and she doesn't know what someone with autism needs."

That was also true. But Abby was finished with dogs. She had other responsibilities now.

"I'm sorry," she told Chris. "I just don't have time to work with Bella."

"I understand," said Chris. "But before you make a final decision, will you do me one favor?"

"What is it?" asked Abby.

"Come to the Helping Paws Center tomorrow. There's somebody I'd like you to meet."

Chapter Eleven

Abby pushed open the glass doors to the waiting room of the Helping Paws Center. At one end of the large, high-ceilinged room was a reception desk, and at the other end was the sensory playground. It had all kinds of interesting stuff that you rarely saw on regular playgrounds. There was a ball pit, a giant rope hammock, and a step pyramid made from the same resilient foam as a gymnastics mat.

Abby's favorite part was a giant keyboard that ran along one wall. Each key played a different note when you stepped on it, and multicolored lights flashed.

Abby saw Chris talking to a young couple at the far end of the room. A few feet away, a small boy was stacking a pile of wooden blocks to make a tower. He wore a white helmet on his head that looked like a bike helmet.

Abby walked over to Chris. "Hi," she said. "My dad dropped me off. He'll be back in an hour, after he does some errands."

"Abby, this is Sam and Lily Sullivan, and their son, Gabe," said Chris. "I've been telling them about you and Amigo."

The man and woman smiled at Abby. They both had lines under their eyes like they were tired.

"Nice to meet you," said Abby. "Hi, Gabe."

Gabe didn't answer or look up at her.

"Gabe is three years old," said Chris. "He was diagnosed with autism last year."

"He doesn't really like to play with other kids," Gabe's mom said to Abby. "But he was really interested in the dog at his cousins' house when we went to visit. That's why we thought a service dog might help him."

Gabe placed another block on the tower, which now rose above his head. The tower began to lean to one side and then fell over with a clatter. With an angry shout, Gabe got to his feet and started hitting his head against the wall nearby.

"Let's play over here, Gabe," said his dad, pulling him away. He handed Gabe a big inflatable ball to play with instead. Abby could see why Gabe was wearing the helmet now.

Gabe ran after the ball as it rolled around the room. He still didn't pay any attention to his parents, Chris, or Abby.

She had a strange feeling as she watched him. It reminded her of her life before Amigo. Abby's memories from that time were different—partly because she had been so young and partly because she hadn't talked then.

Abby didn't have many memories about people she'd met when she was little. She remembered things in her environment: the dark coat cubby in her kindergarten classroom where she liked to hide, the pattern of the plaid fabric on the living room couch, the dusty driveway where she liked to go outside and count all the rocks until she couldn't count any higher.

She also remembered that the world had seemed loud and frightening then. Lights were too bright; sounds were too loud. People asked her things she didn't understand or told her to do things she didn't want to do. She remembered her parents' voices, and Natalie's, but not really their faces.

It was hard to say exactly how Amigo had changed that. Somehow, she'd just felt calmer and happier when he was around. Before, it was almost like Abby had been a caterpillar curled up in a tight ball to protect herself. With Amigo at her side, she had relaxed enough to begin exploring the world around her.

Gabe was stacking the blocks again. His mom walked up beside him and tried to get him to look at a storybook she wanted to read to him. Gabe looked briefly at the cartoon characters on the page, his expression blank. Then he picked up another block and set it on top of the pile.

"Your tower is seventeen blocks high," Abby said to Gabe. "That's very impressive."

Gabe didn't seem to hear her. He probably did, though. He just thought the blocks were more interesting.

Sometimes, Abby thought that her books or computer games or making a pattern out of colored pencils were more interesting than having a conversation too. Sometimes, she compromised by talking to people when she didn't really feel like it. Other times, she went into her Cave of Solitude or the chill-out chair so she could be alone. It was easy for her to spend hours looking at the pattern of a seashell or standing outside with her eyes closed, feeling the grass under her feet.

When Abby had first gotten Amigo, she'd spent a lot of time just stroking and brushing his fur. She remembered how soft and warm it felt. But gradually, she started to notice that Amigo was more than just fur and a licking tongue. He reacted to things that she did. He was interested in her—and everyone else around him.

When Abby was with him, she noticed all the things Amigo noticed and all the people around her who wanted to get to know Amigo, and Abby too.

She remembered the day that Miriam had come up to her at recess and asked to pet Amigo. They had been friends ever since. And they were still friends. Abby had been worried after Caleb and Miriam left the memorial service, but Miriam hadn't been mad at all.

"I could see that you were overwhelmed," she'd said when Abby had finally worked up the courage to talk to her. "Caleb and I left because we thought you needed some space. Anyway, it *is* kind of a cheesy poem. I just wanted you to know that I was thinking about you."

Abby looked over at Gabe now. She hoped that someday, he might be able to make as good a friend as Miriam. But right now, he was so focused on the wooden blocks that he couldn't make any friends at all.

Abby tugged on Chris's sleeve. She walked with

him a short distance away, over to the giant keyboard. She stepped on the first key, and it played a low note.

Sometimes, it was easier for Abby to communicate if she was moving. As she said what she wanted to say to Chris, she jumped on a new key with each word.

"I. Think. Bella. Can. Help. Gabe," she said. She was halfway across the keyboard. She wasn't a hundred percent sure about what she wanted to say next, but she jumped onto the next key anyway. It let out a high, clear note.

"I . . ." Abby began. She closed her eyes, bent her knees, and then leaped to the next key. "Can." *Jump.* "Help." *Jump.* "You." *Jump.* "Train." *Jump.* "Bella."

Abby had reached the end of the keyboard. She looked up at Chris, whose face lit up. "That's great, Abby!" he said. "I think you'll know better than anyone how to work with her."

Abby heard the sound of barking from the other room and looked over at the door to the kennel room. "Do you want to meet the guide dogs that I'm training now?" asked Chris.

Abby hesitated. It felt like Amigo's absence had left a big hole in her life. It was too big to be filled by other dogs, but letting it stay completely empty felt worse. It felt almost like the time before Amigo.

"Okay," said Abby.

They said goodbye to Gabe's parents before they headed into the kennel. Abby made sure to say goodbye to Gabe, too, but he didn't look up from his tower of blocks.

Abby sat cross-legged in her Cave of Solitude. The blue-green light shining through the tent walls illuminated the photograph she held in her hand. It was Abby's school picture from last year. Amigo was with her, wearing his service dog vest. He looked alert and proud sitting beside her.

Abby put the photo down and picked up another. This one was of her and Amigo playing in a big pile of autumn leaves. Another showed Amigo in his tuxedo at the county fair Natalie had mentioned in her memorial speech.

It was the first time Abby had looked at the pictures since Amigo died. It was the first time she had let herself really think about what her life would be like, now that he was gone.

Whenever Abby thought about Bella, Destiny, or another dog, she felt like she was being disloyal to Amigo's memory. But when Amigo was alive, he had never been jealous of the time Abby had spent with other dogs on the ranch. Why should things be any different now that he was gone?

The other problem was that being around other dogs was just too painful. They all reminded her of

Amigo, but none of them were him. Abby had made an exception for Bella only because she wanted to help Gabe.

But was avoiding dogs completely really the best solution? Abby wasn't any happier feeding ferrets and mucking out horse stalls. Dogs were the animals she loved best. *All* dogs.

The day before, Abby had met Lucy and Milo, the guide dogs Chris was training. At first, her heart had sunk when she'd seen that Milo was a golden retriever that looked a lot like Amigo. But his personality was totally different from Amigo's. Abby had closed her eyes, pretending for a moment that she was blind. She let Milo lead her around the room, helping her avoid all the obstacles in her path.

Last week, someone had dropped off a new litter of puppies at Second Chance Ranch. It was impossible to tell what their breed was. They were a jumble of floppy ears and pointy ears, short tails and long tails, wiry coats and smooth. Grace and Emily couldn't stop fussing over them. But now that Grace did all the dog work, Abby had hardly gotten to see them.

If only I had traded chores with Emily instead of Grace, Abby thought wistfully. Emily would probably switch back with her just to be nice. But Grace? Not so likely.

Earlier that day, Abby and Grace had gotten into another argument. Grace had been playing her karaoke video game on the living room TV, while Abby was trying to watch a documentary about the history of service animals in her room. She'd learned that guide dogs were first used after World War I, when many soldiers had been blinded by poisonous gas.

But then she couldn't learn anything else, because the sound of Grace's voice screeching along to the rock music was so distracting. She'd gone downstairs and told Grace that she sounded just like Daisy, the Berkshire pig, when she'd gotten stuck in the narrow space between his feed trough and the shed wall.

Grace had stormed off to her room and slammed the door behind her. As far as Abby knew, she was still there.

If Abby ever wanted her old chores back, she'd have to make peace with Grace. She climbed out of the tent and headed down the hall to the bedroom Grace and Emily shared. A rhythmic *thump*, *thump*, *thump* sound came from inside.

Abby knocked on the door.

Grace's muffled voice said, "What?"

Abby took that as permission to enter.

Grace was lying on her bed, throwing a bouncy ball at the ceiling and then catching it as it sprang back toward her hands. Chances was stretched out next to Grace on the bed. She blinked lazily at Abby, and Abby resisted the urge to stick out her tongue at the cat.

Even though Abby fed her now, Chances still went out of her way to make Abby's life difficult. She always disappeared at mealtimes and made Abby track her down. She shed white fur all over Abby's favorite black sweatshirt and chewed the corner off her ecosystem poster. Abby had had to explain to Mr. Timothy that a *cat* had eaten her homework.

"Oh, it's you," said Grace when she saw Abby. She started bouncing her ball again. "Couldn't find any other sisters to criticize?"

Abby figured that she had better get Grace into a better mood before she made any kind of request.

"I'm sorry about what I said earlier," said Abby, watching the progress of the ball as it ricocheted from the ceiling to Grace's outstretched hands. It was pretty impressive that Grace managed to catch it every time.

"Your singing is . . ." Abby couldn't think of an honest compliment. "Something you enjoy," she said finally. "Comparing it to the squealing of a pig was rude." *But accurate*, she thought.

Grace's eyes narrowed. She caught the ball again, and this time, held it clenched in her hand. "But it's not just today," she said. "You're always getting mad at me for practically no reason."

"I already said I was sorry for calling you Hurricane Grace."

"What about that time you yelled at me for

knocking over Emily's colored pencils?" Grace demanded. "That was rude, too, and you never apologized."

"Okay, I'm sorry for that too," said Abby. "You do mess up a lot of things, but to say that you ruin literally everything is an exaggeration."

Grace glared at Abby with her eyes narrowed and her lips pressed into a tight line. It was an angry face, for sure. The apology didn't seem to be working.

"There are a lot of things I like about you, actually," Abby continued.

"Yeah? Like what?"

"Um . . . you're a good soccer player."

"What else?" asked Grace.

"Most other sports too."

"And?"

"I'm sure there are other things. I just can't think of them right now."

"Uh-huh." Grace rolled her eyes. "What do you want, anyway?"

"I wanted to know if we can switch back our chores again."

Grace rubbed her chin. "Hmm," she said thoughtfully. "Playing with the puppies is a lot more fun than getting bitten by that ferret and cleaning Joker's stall."

"But I'm better at training dogs than you are," said Abby, who was starting to feel annoyed again.

As soon as the words left her mouth, she knew they were the wrong thing to say. Grace's eyebrows shot up, and her arms folded across her chest.

"No, I think I like the arrangement we have now," said Grace. A mischievous smirk crossed her face. "Joker needs to get his dose of deworming medication this week," she added. "You're going to have a great time holding him while Natalie tries to squirt the paste down his throat."

"No, I'm not!" cried Abby. Then she recognized the sarcasm in Grace's voice. She sighed. It sounded like she would be playing a lot more games of hide-and-seek with Chances.

"Okay," she said sadly and turned to leave the room.

"Hey, wait a minute!" Grace called out from behind her. "Aren't you even going to try to negotiate?"

Abby spun back around, her forehead furrowed with confusion. "What do you mean?" she asked.

"I mean, like, if you were to give me a good *reason* to switch back, maybe I'd consider it." Grace held up her bouncy ball between her thumb and forefinger. She squinted at it from different angles, as if she were examining a valuable gem.

"Because I want you to," said Abby.

Grace shook her head. Abby shrugged, totally lost.

"How about because you're going to do my math homework for a month?" Grace suggested with a grin.

"I can't do your homework for you," said Abby. "That's cheating."

"You can check the answers," Grace replied. "And if they're wrong, you can help me correct them."

Abby really wanted to work with the dogs again.

"Fine," she agreed. "But you better actually learn the lessons. I can't take your tests for you."

"Yeah, yeah," said Grace. "So do we have a deal?"

Abby held out her hand, and they shook on it. She left the bedroom, and a moment later, she heard the *bounce, bounce, bounce* of Grace's ball again.

Sisters . . . thought Abby, shaking her head. *If only I could live with a nice pack of wolves instead.*

Chapter Twelve

"Heel, Bella," said Abby as Bella strained against her collar. She wanted to greet a couple teenagers with rainbow-colored haircuts in front of a kiosk that sold jewelry at the mall. The teenagers laughed and patted Bella before Abby managed to drag her away.

"Heel" meant that Bella was supposed to walk quietly at Abby's side, without too much tension on the leash. Right now, Bella was definitely not heeling. She was out in front of Abby with her tail wagging furiously. She was so excited by their outing that she dragged Abby along behind her like a Siberian husky pulling a sled in the Iditarod.

It had been a month since Abby had agreed to help train Bella. Already, Bella was getting better at following basic commands like "sit," "stay," "come," "lie down," and "heel." Or, at least, she was better at home.

A big part of Bella's training as a service dog would involve teaching her to pay attention to her handler in public places. If Bella were eventually going to go to school with Gabe, she would need to remember her training in noisy and distracting situations.

Abby had thought the perfect place to practice would be the Sassafras Springs Mall, just one town over. It was filled with people and tempting sights, sounds, and smells.

Mrs. Ramirez had agreed to drive Abby and Bella to the mall while she did some errands. She was a short distance ahead, getting the cracked screen on her cell phone replaced at the electronics store.

Natalie had come too. She was supposed to be keeping an eye on Abby and Bella, but they'd lost her awhile back. Abby looked over her shoulder and saw her sister behind her, standing in front of a display of calendars and flipping through the ones with pictures of horses. That was classic Natalie—if there was a horse anywhere around, or even a photo of one, everybody in the mall could be replaced by giant talking iguanas and she probably wouldn't notice.

A woman with a fancy manicure and arms loaded with shopping bags looked curiously at Bella as she walked past. Bella was wearing an orange vest that said "Service Dog in Training."

Abby had gotten the vest from Chris so that Bella could practice being out in public. It was the law that service dogs had to be allowed in public places. At the end of her training, Chris would give Bella the Public Access Test. Passing it would allow Bella to go with Gabe anywhere—even on an airplane.

At this point, though, Abby just hoped she and Bella would get through the trip without breaking something expensive she'd have to pay for! She cringed as Bella bumped into a rotating display of sunglasses and sent it spinning in crazy circles.

They passed a toy store next. The mother of the toddler whom Bella greeted coming out of the toy store wasn't as easygoing as the teenagers had been.

"Control your dog!" the woman snapped, pulling her child protectively out of the way.

"Sorry," said Abby, hurrying Bella along. She paused to regroup in front of the empty storefront of a gift shop that had gone out of business.

"Sit, Bella," said Abby. A little obedience work would help focus Bella's attention. But Bella was looking in the other direction. Her nose wafted the air as a man walked past, carrying a slice of pepperoni pizza on a paper plate.

Abby gave the leash a tug to get Bella's attention and repeated the command. Bella immediately sank down onto her haunches.

"Good girl," said Abby. "Now lie down."

A shadow fell across Abby's path. She looked up and saw a tall, broad-shouldered security officer. His uniform looked like a police uniform. A set of hand-cuffs dangled from his belt.

The officer stared down at Bella. " 'Service Dog in Training,' huh?" he said.

Abby gulped. Bella wasn't certified yet, so the law that allowed service dogs to be in public places didn't technically apply to her. She'd been hoping

Bella would behave well enough that no one would question her presence.

"That's right," said Abby in a small voice. "We're practicing for the Public Access Test."

"Well, I've had a complaint from a shopper about this dog. Do you have a parent or guardian with you today?"

Abby pointed across the mall's wide aisle to the electronics store. Her mom was still arguing with the sales associate, pointing at her receipt. The officer went over to speak with her, and a moment later, Mrs. Ramirez hurried over.

"Is it true that Bella tried to bite a toddler?" she asked, a concerned look on her face.

"No!" said Abby. "She tried to *lick* a toddler."

"Oh, I see," said Mrs. Ramirez. "That makes more sense. But we still have to leave now. Maybe it wasn't the best idea to bring her here today . . ."

"But Bella needs to get exposure to all kinds of situations," Abby reminded her as they headed over to the calendar stand, where Natalie was still entranced by images of Arabians, Thoroughbreds, and Clydesdales.

"Just . . . maybe not quite yet," Abby added, yanking the corner of a pocket calendar out of Bella's mouth. "I guess we need to spend a little more time on the basics first."

Chapter Thirteen

Abby took a deep breath as she stood outside the Helping Paws Center. She could see Gabe and his family through the glass doors.

Abby looked down as Bella nudged her hand, probably wondering why they were just standing there. But she waited quietly instead of prancing in circles around Abby or trying to drag her through the door.

She had made a lot of progress in the past month. Chris thought that Bella was ready to meet Gabe. They wouldn't know for sure if Bella and Gabe were right for each other until they spent time together.

Now that the moment had come, Abby felt her confidence fading. Bella could still get carried away sometimes. *What if she forgets her manners and jumps on Gabe? What if Gabe is afraid of her?*

Abby pushed the fears out of her mind. Everyone was waiting for her. She opened the door and led Bella through it.

She waved hello to Chris, who was sitting on the floor with Gabe. His parents came over and crouched down in front of Bella. They stroked her thick black fur as Bella licked them and pranced happily in place.

"She seems so sweet and loving," said Gabe's mom, cupping Bella's chin in her hand.

"She is," said Abby. She showed them how Bella could walk on the leash without pulling ahead or stopping to sniff at objects she passed. She asked Bella to "Sit" and then "Lie down."

Then she said, "Stay, Bella." She dropped the leash and walked to the other end of the room. "Stay" was the hardest command for Bella. She wanted to be where the action was. Her whole body tensed up as she resisted the urge to jump to her feet.

Abby made sure that her body language was consistent with her command. She kept her palm raised slightly in Bella's direction and held her body a little bit stiffly. She avoided making eye contact while she slowly counted to ten in her head.

"Good stay," Abby praised Bella after the seconds had passed. "Now come here!"

Bella didn't need to be asked twice. She leaped up and raced over to Abby. But she didn't jump on her. Instead, she skidded to a stop a few feet away and sat down without being asked. Her eyes were bright and her ears alert, waiting for the next signal.

"Abby, I'm really impressed," said Chris. "I've never seen a dog learn basic obedience so quickly. I'm sure she'll be ready to learn service dog tasks in no time."

Abby flushed, pleased and slightly embarrassed by the compliment. To her, working with Bella was as natural as having a conversation.

"Should we introduce Bella to Gabe now?" asked Chris.

Abby's heart beat faster, and her palms started to sweat. Leading Bella by her leash, she followed Chris over to the corner where Gabe was playing.

"Look, Gabe," said his mother. "This puppy wants to meet you."

Today, Gabe was lining up a row of cars and trucks in order from largest to smallest. He looked up briefly at Bella and Abby, and then turned back to his task. Abby saw Gabe's mom and dad exchange unhappy glances.

Bella reached out and put her paw on the toy dump truck that Gabe was about to add to the lineup. Gabe looked up at Bella, his mouth falling open slightly with surprise. For a minute, the two of them stared deeply into each other's eyes.

Gabe's eyes got wide, and his mouth twitched. For a minute, Abby thought he was going to start crying. Then he threw back his head and laughed. He laughed so hard that he rolled onto his side and then his back, kicking his legs in the air. Bella rolled onto her side, too, her mouth panting open with delight.

That made Gabe laugh even harder. The sound of it made Abby laugh too, even though she wasn't sure exactly what Gabe thought was so funny. She looked over at Gabe's parents and was startled to see that both of them had tears in their eyes.

"What's the matter?" she asked, her fears rushing back. "Did Bella do something wrong?"

"No," said Gabe's mom. She looked over at Bella and Gabe, who were still rolling around on the floor together. "It's just that we've never heard Gabe laugh before."

"Does that mean you want Bella to have a home with Gabe when she's ready?" asked Abby.

"Yes," said Gabe's dad. "Bella will have a home with us forever."

Abby felt a flush of pride and happiness. All her hard work had paid off. Then, as the words echoed in her head, sadness settled over her again.

"Forever . . ." Abby had thought that Amigo would be with her forever. But it had only been four years. Even though Bella was just a puppy, her life would still be shorter than Gabe's.

It's not fair that dogs have less time to live than people do, thought Abby. But she wouldn't have traded her time with Amigo for anything, even though it hadn't been nearly long enough.

Amigo had changed Abby's life so much that, in a way, almost everything she said or did was because of him. She was training Bella, using the skills that Amigo had taught her. And Bella would use the training Abby gave her to help Gabe. So in a way, Amigo was helping Gabe too.

Now Abby thought she understood what Natalie

had meant when she'd said, "Amigo might be gone, but he's still with us in our hearts." Amigo was never really gone as long as people remembered and loved him. And that was the closest thing to forever that she could imagine.

About the Author

Whitney Sanderson grew up riding horses as a member of a 4-H club and competing in local jumping and dressage shows. She has written several books in the Horse Diaries chapter book series. She is also the author of *Horse Rescue: Treasure*, based on her time volunteering at an equine rescue farm. She lives in Massachusetts.

About the Illustrator

Jomike Tejido is an author and illustrator who has illustrated the books *I Funny: School of Laughs* and *Middle School: Dog's Best Friend*, as well as the Pet Charms and I Want to Be . . . Dinosaurs! series. He has fond memories of horseback riding as a kid and has always liked drawing fluffy animals. Jomike lives in Manila with his wife, two daughters, and a chow chow named Oso.

When Buddy, the class rabbit, goes missing, Emily is distraught. It was her responsibility to take care of Buddy over spring break, and now he is gone. The angry glares from her classmates don't help her blues either. The only bright spot is her new friend Oliver. But as Emily's friendship with Oliver blossoms, the possibility of finding Buddy withers away. Can Emily recover from the loss of Buddy?

When Natalie saves enough money to buy
Apocalypse, she's certain she has found her heart
horse: a horse that's so special it's as if they're a
part of your heart. She hopes he's the horse to
help her win a barrel-racing title too. But Eleven
arrives at the ranch the same day as Apocalypse.
Eleven suffered abuse and needs proper care.
Natalie finds herself caring for Eleven when she
should be barrel racing with Apocalypse. Will
Natalie become a barrel-racing champion? Which
horse will truly capture her heart?

KELSEY ABRAMS

HEART HORSE

ILLUSTRATED BY JOMIKE TEJIDO

A NATALIE
STORY

SECOND CHANCE
RANCH

Life at Second Chance Ranch becomes hectic after Grace offers to take in animals from a petting zoo. Even though her impulsiveness earns her the responsibility of taking care of the big Berkshire pig, Daisy, she is happy that the llama, Harry, is also under her care . . . that is, until she discovers his ill temper. Still, she decides to train Harry as part of her science project. But spitting llamas don't care if a hypothesis is proven or not. Can Grace pull off the best science project ever?

Join Natalie, Abby, Emily, and Grace and
read more animal stories in . . .

SECOND CHANCE
RANCH

BY KELSEY ABRAMS

ILLUSTRATED BY JOMIKE TEJIDO

CHARMING MIDDLE GRADE FICTION
FROM JOLLY FISH PRESS

JOLLY
FiSH
PRESS